To Bilal,
Enjoy all the winter fun!
Sharon Debowski
2017

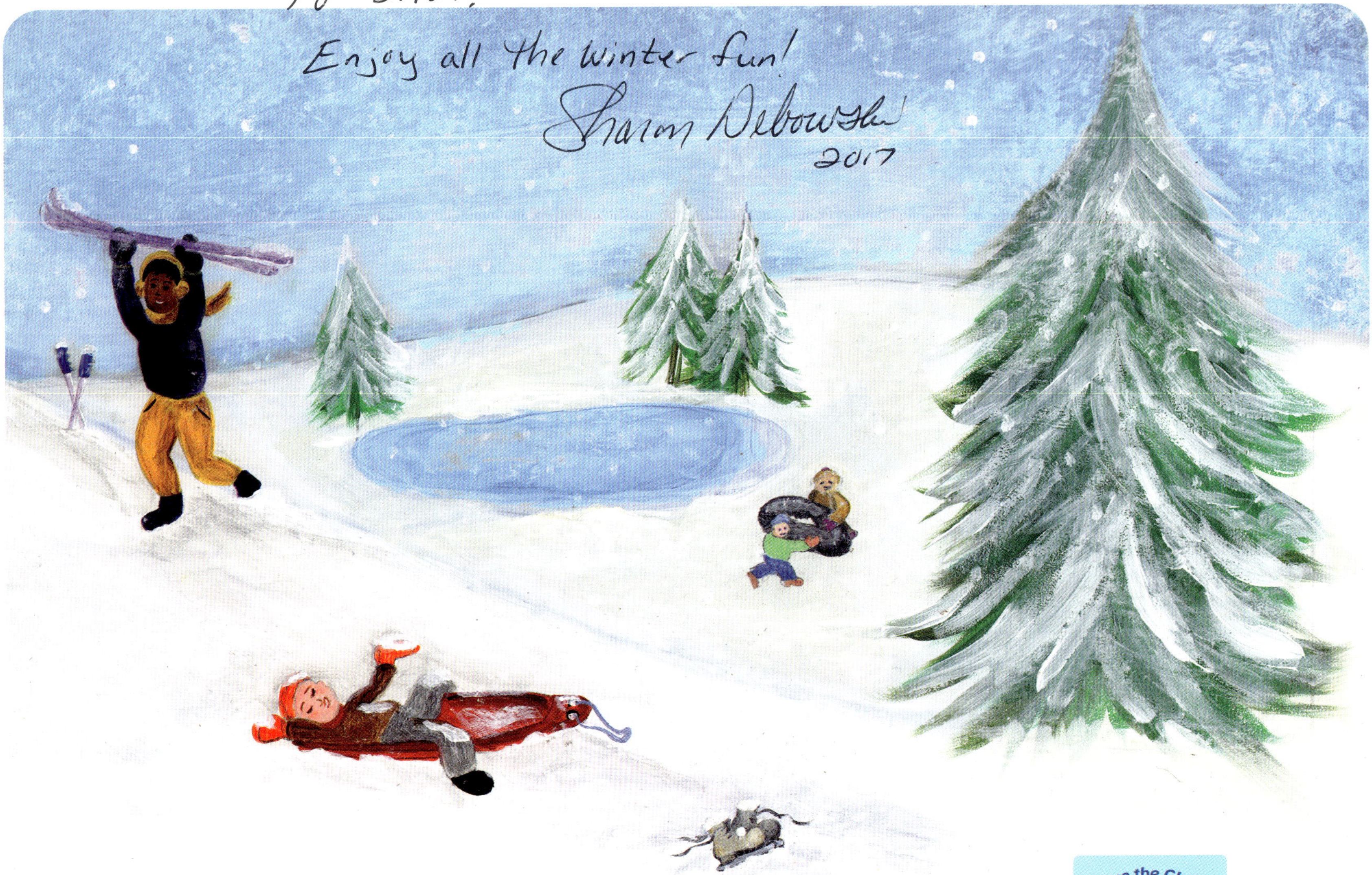

By Sharon Debowski

Illustrated by Inger Sommer Eadie and Debi Grimm

New Jersey

Many thanks to Pamela Pollack, Sylvia Frezzolini, and Arlene Goldberg for sharing their knowledge and experience and to Alfred Giuliani for his wonderful digital enhancements to the art.

Thank you to the teachers at Byram Lakes Elementary School who gave me their honest opinions and encouragement.

Text and illustrations copyright © 2007 by Sharon Debowski

Above the Clouds Publishing, P.O. Box 313, Stanhope, N.J. 07874

Library of Congress Cataloging-in-Publication Data
Debowski, Sharon, 1964-
The snowman, the owl, and the groundhog / by Sharon Debowski ; illustrated by Inger Sommer Eadie and Debi Grimm. -- 1st ed. p. cm.
Summary: A snowman tries to prolong winter by offering his hat and scarf to prevent a groundhog from seeing his shadow, but Owl and Groundhog help him to appreciate what he has, rather than worrying about the future.
ISBN 978-1-60227-470-9 (hardcover : alk. paper)
[1. Contentment--Fiction. 2. Snowmen--Fiction. 3. Owls--Fiction. 4. Woodchuck--Fiction. 5. Winter--Fiction. 6. Stories in rhyme.] I. Eadie, Inger Sommer, ill. II. Grimm, Debi, ill. III. Title.

PZ8.3.D356Sno 2007
[E]--dc22
2006036289
ISBN-13: 978-1-60227-470-9
ISBN-10: 1-60227-470-3 / First Edition: 2007
1 3 5 7 9 10 8 6 4 2

Book design by Arlene Schleifer Goldberg
Printed in the U.S.A. by Newburyport Press

There are eight bunnies throughout the book, can you find them all?

This book is dedicated to
Harmony and Logan

and to my father,
who instilled in me a love of reading

The snow started falling in early December.
At least, that's what the snowman remembers.

The children came outside to play.
"Let's build a snowman," they did say.

They made him out of three giant snowballs.
He was so tall he towered over them all.

The children visited day after day.
They admired the snowman from every which way.

They waved to him, so stately and still, whenever they pulled their sleds up the hill.

One day the snowman heard the children say, "Springtime will be here any day!"

"Springtime? Springtime? What could it be? What will the new season bring for me?" Snowman wondered.

Snowman asked Groundhog, "Is it true what they say? When it gets warm, winter goes away?"

"It's true," Groundhog said. "Spring is drawing near. Some say it's if I see my shadow appear."

The snowy owl flew down from her tree.
She said, "My dear snowman, listen to me.

There's no need to worry. There's no need to fret.
Winter's far from over yet."

"But if it's true, I will melt!" Snowman cried, all bereft.
"My nose, buttons, and hat will be all that is left!"
Snowman spoke to Groundhog,
"I'll give you my broom and my scarf and my hat.
Just don't look for your shadow. It's as easy as that!"

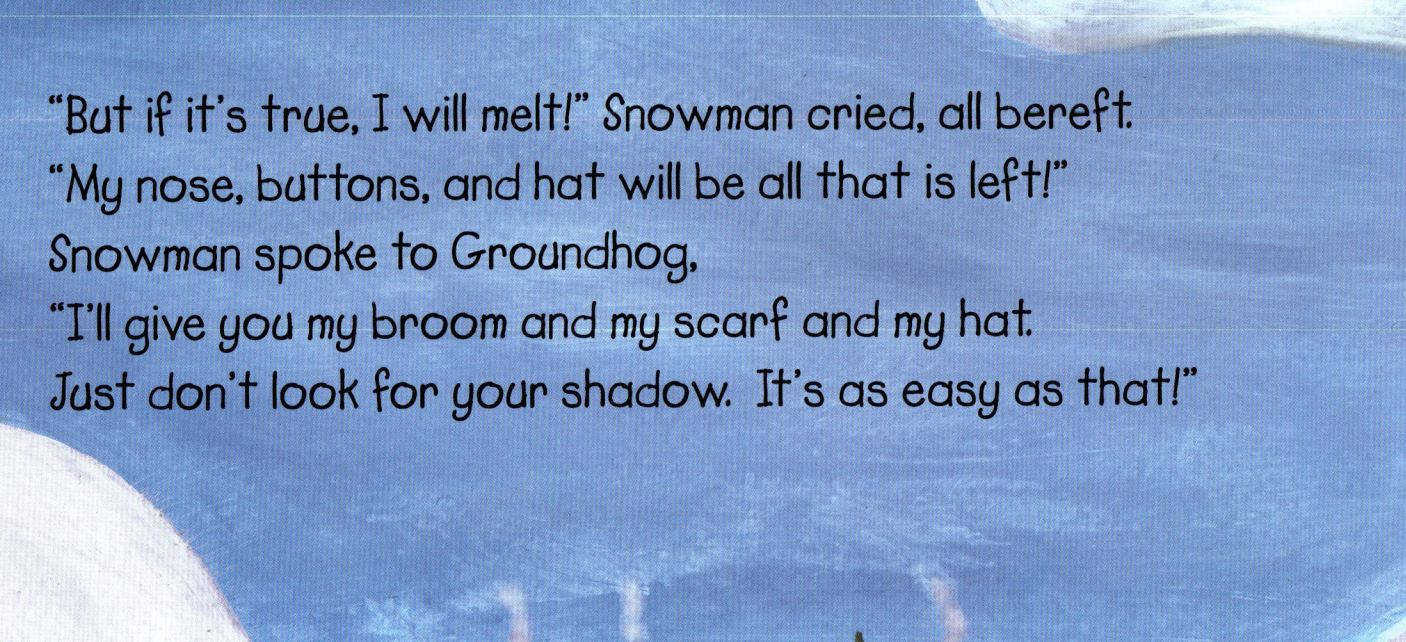

"Children built you in winter,"
Owl said, "out of snow.
But spring is the time
for the flowers to grow."

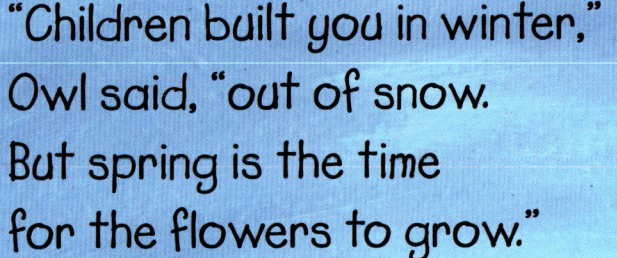

Then Groundhog said,
"My staying home won't stop the spring.
The seasons don't stop for anything."

"In summer when the sky is a brighter blue,
they'll sip lemonade and remember you."

Groundhog climbed back into his den.
"Perhaps, in time, I will see you again.
I may see my shadow, then again I may not.
You have to remember the good things you've got.
You have children who love you, and you made them glad.
Remember," said Groundhog, "not to be sad."

The next day dawned, it was cloudy and cold.
Snowman tried to remember what he'd been told.
The children came out and looked all around.
Snow began to fall from the sky to the ground.

Bunny asked Snowman, "What will you do?"
Snowman answered, "With all this fresh snow, I'll feel brand new!"
He picked up his broom without hesitating.
There were games to play, and the children were waiting.

The snowman knew winter would come to an end.
But next winter the children would rebuild their friend.
Where would they build him? He started to think.
Maybe in the middle of the giant ice rink.